Don't go to School!

written by Máire Zepf

illustrated by Tarsila Krüse

Futa Fata

To Lorcán, Cillian and Áine – three stars who went to school very happily – Máire

To Eric and Otto, who both made me Mom – Tarsila

First Published in 2015 by
Futa Fata
An Spidéal,
Co na Gaillimhe,
Ireland,
under the title *Ná Gabh ar Scoil!*

This English-Language edition © 2018 Futa Fata
Original text © 2015–2018 Máire Zepf
Illustrations © 2015–2018 Tarsila Krüse
Cover and book design: Anú Design, Tara

Adapted from the original Irish by the author

ISBN: 978-1-910945-38-4

Futa Fata

"It's morning!" cried Benno. "Today is my big day!"

Benno got dressed in his new school clothes.
He looked very smart indeed.

"Mummy!" he called, "Get up!
I can't be late for school on my very first day!"

Next, he ate his favourite breakfast.

He put on his brand new coat.
He was REALLY excited!
He only had one problem.

It was Mummy.

"Don't go to school!" she wailed.

"Stay here with me, Benno!"

Benno spoke to her softly.
"New things are a little scary
sometimes, Mummy.
But you'll be fine when you're there.
Wait and see."

Benno gave Mummy a big hug
and off they went to school, hand in hand.

Mummy looked around the schoolyard.
"Let's go home, Benno," she said. "I don't know anyone here!"

"Don't worry, Mummy," said Benno. "You'll get to know the other parents in no time. They seem really nice!"

"Good morning!" said the teacher, "I'm Mrs Nolan."

"Welcome! Come inside and see the classroom.
Don't be shy – we're all friendly here!"

Before long, Mummy was as happy as could be. She really enjoyed the sandbox. And the kitchen corner was even more fun!

"Painting!" she cried. "I love painting!"

"Mummy, you are too big for school," Benno told her.
"You have to go home now."

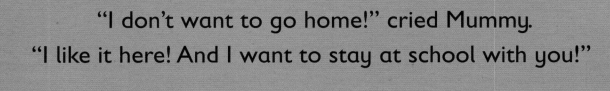

"I don't want to go home!" cried Mummy.
"I like it here! And I want to stay at school with you!"

Benno had an idea. He kissed his own hands and filled Mummy's pocket with the kisses. "If you miss me during the day, put your hand in your pocket and pull out a kiss. Then you'll feel my love for you, even when we aren't together."

Mummy felt better.
She headed for home.
Benno was happy too.
He knew that Mummy
would be all right now.

"Time to dance!"
said the teacher.

"I love school!" Benno laughed.
He played and played with his
new friends.

What a surprise when he heard the
'ding a ling a ling' of the bell.
It was time to go home already!

Outside, Mummy was waiting for Benno.
Benno gave her a huge hug. "You were so brave, Mummy!"

"Everything will be easier for you tomorrow –
just wait and see." said Benno.

"Tomorrow?" said Mummy in shock.
"Don't tell me you'll be going to school again tomorrow!"